My Voice Is a Trumpet

written by

PLATINUM-SELLING COUNTRY MUSIC ARTIST

JIMMIE ALLEN

illustrated by

CATHY ANN JOHNSON

FLAMINGO
BOOKS

FLAMINGO BOOKS
An imprint of Penguin Random House LLC, New York

First published in the United States of America by Flamingo Books,
an imprint of Penguin Random House LLC, 2021

Flamingo Books & colophon are registered trademarks
of Penguin Random House LLC.

Visit us online at penguinrandomhouse.com.

LIBRARY OF CONGRESS CATALOGING-IN-PUBLICATION DATA IS AVAILABLE.

Printed in the United States of America

ISBN 9780593352182

10   9   8   7   6   5   4   3   2   1

Book design by Cathy Ann Johnson and Jim Hoover
Text set in Arbutus Slab

Some have a voice
AS TALL AS A TREE—

LOUD and PROUD

and sways in the breeze.

Some have a voice as small as a bee, soft and sweet like KISSES OF HONEY.

Some have a voice that's
PATIENT and WISE ...

with LESSONS OF LIFE told
through sparkling eyes.

Some have a voice
sunny and bright,
a voice that can echo and
LIGHT UP THE NIGHT.

There's a voice that is silent
but STILL CAN BE HEARD
with hands that move
to speak EVERY word.

Then there's the voice that
ROARS like a lion,
a big voice that tells you—
ALWAYS KEEP TRYIN'!

We ALL have voices, voices to hear.
MY VOICE IS A TRUMPET—strong and clear.

My voice WILL BE LOUD
when I'm not sure I know.

To WONDER, to LEARN,
and to ASK as I go.

I will learn to **SPEAK UP**
to show I am strong,
TO STAND FOR WHAT'S RIGHT,
and to know what feels wrong.

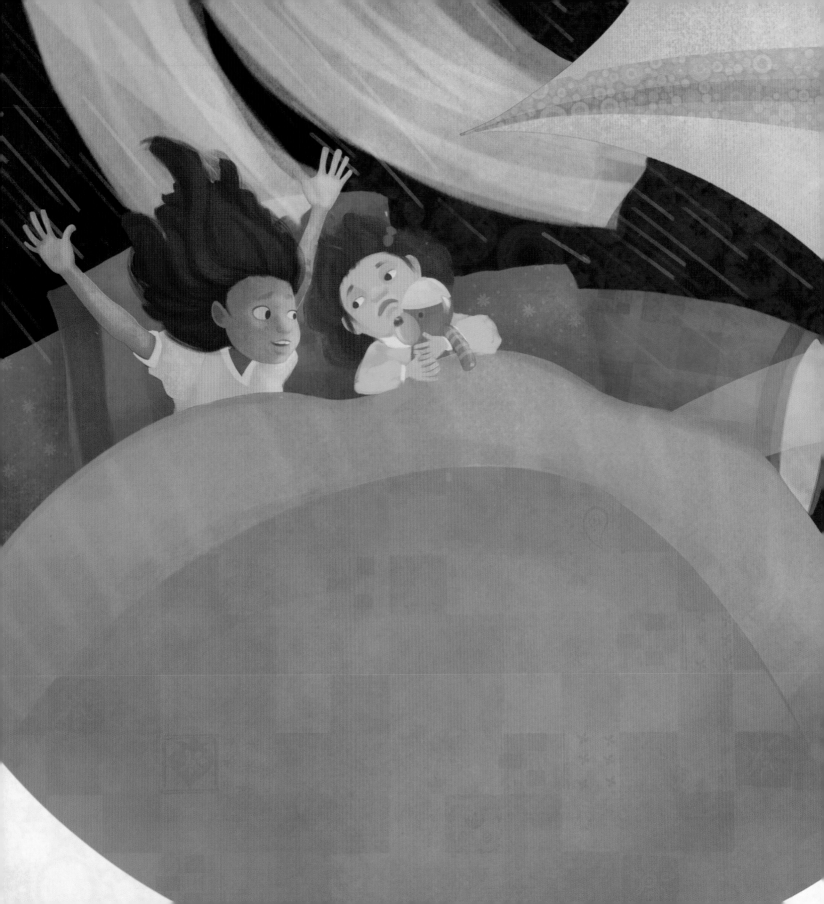

My voice is a rainbow after the storm, loving, comforting, **SAFE,** and warm.

I'll use my voice
to find joy in others,
reminding us **ALL**
we're **SISTERS**
and BROTHERS.

I'LL SAY NO TO HATE
by using this voice,
and **ALWAYS CHOOSE LOVE—**
a magical choice.

VOICES ARE POWERFUL,
and together they're strong,
like the musical notes of
a BEAUTIFUL song.

Bullies

How will *you* use YOUR VOICE?